Please help the bunnies of Moonglow Meadow!

Our brave and loyal friend, Arrow, has traveled far from our world to protect the magic key that keeps our kingdom safe from the dark rabbits. Arrow is very far from home and will need your help.

Could you be his friend?

This magic bunny might be hard to spot as he is very small and often appears in different fluffy bunny disguises—but you can recognize him by the rainbow twinkle in his eyes.

lp!

ke

Leader of Moonglow Meadow

To Nirvana, so sweet.

Baby, you're the best—SB

GROSSET & DUNLAP
Published by the Penguin Group
Penguin Group (USA) LLC, 375 Hudson Street, New York, New York 10014, USA

USA | Canada | UK | Ireland | Australia | New Zealand | India | South Africa | China

penguin.com
A Penguin Random House Company

Text copyright © 2010 Sue Bentley. Illustrations copyright © 2010 Angela Swan. Cover illustration © 2010 Andrew Farley. First published in Great Britain in 2010 by Puffin Books. First published in the United States in 2014 by Grosset & Dunlap, a division of Penguin Young Readers Group, 345 Hudson Street, New York, New York 10014. GROSSET & DUNLAP is a trademark of Penguin Group (USA) LLC. Printed in the U.S.A.

Library of Congress Cataloging-in-Publication Data is available.

ISBN 978-0-448-46793-1   10 9 8 7 6 5 4 3 2 1

Magic Bunny

Dancing Days

SUE BENTLEY

illustrated by Angela Swan

Grosset & Dunlap
An Imprint of Penguin Group (USA) LLC

Prologue

Arrow jumped into the air and happily kicked out his back legs as he looked around at Moonglow Meadow. His silky white fur, flecked with silver, gleamed in the moonlight. Tiny rainbows shone in his warm brown eyes. It felt good to be back.

His fellow magic rabbits were nibbling juicy leaves or gathering around crystal pools to drink. The moon seemed to turn all the brightly colored wild flowers into pale jewels.

The grass smelled delicious, and Arrow began to eat. The tiny key he wore on a fine chain around his neck tinkled faintly.

Arrow saw a movement from the corner of his eye. An older rabbit with a wise expression and a dark gray muzzle was bounding toward him.

"Strike!" Arrow stopped eating and bowed his head in greeting before the leader of the warren.

"It is good to see you," Strike said warmly. "Moonglow Meadow is lush and green again because of the key's magic."

As chosen keeper of the magical key, it was Arrow's job to look after it. "I came at once when the key glowed brightly, telling me that more of its magic was needed."

"We are all thankful to you." Strike reached out a paw and touched Arrow's shoulder. "But I have bad news. The dark rabbits are approaching to try to steal the key."

The dark rabbits lived in a deep gully next to Moonglow Meadow. Their land had become so dry that nothing grew there anymore, and they were hungry.

"So they still are unwilling to share our land?" Arrow guessed.

Strike nodded. "They want to use the key's power to make only *their* gully green and beautiful again."

"But then *our* meadow would become a desert!" Arrow said, shocked. "What can we do?"

"You must be brave, Arrow, and go

back to the Otherworld to keep the key safe," Strike said.

Arrow felt very young and afraid as he thought of all the unknown dangers. But he took a deep breath and nodded slowly. "I will go."

Strike smiled with pride and affection. "Well said." Then, lifting his head, he gave a soft but piercing cry.

All the other rabbits in the warren pricked up their ears and came rushing toward them. They formed a circle around Arrow. The golden key glowed as brightly as the sun.

The light slowly faded and where the young pure-white-and-silver rabbit had been, there now sat a tiny fluffy black-and-white bunny with huge chocolate-brown eyes that gleamed with tiny rainbows.

"This disguise will protect you. Only return when we need more of the key's magic," Strike instructed. "And watch out for dark rabbits!"

Arrow drew himself up. "I will not fail the warren!"

Thud. Thud. Thud. The rabbits began thumping their feet in time. Arrow felt the magic building and a cloud of crystal dust shimmered around him, and Moonglow Meadow began to fade . . .

Chapter ONE

Sara Penfold bit back tears as she hobbled across the hospital parking lot.

"Lean on me. That's it." Sara's dad steadied her so she could scoot awkwardly into the backseat of their car. "Okay?" he asked. "At least you'll be able to get around on those crutches the hospital has loaned you. And the doctor says your ankle will soon be as good as new. Things

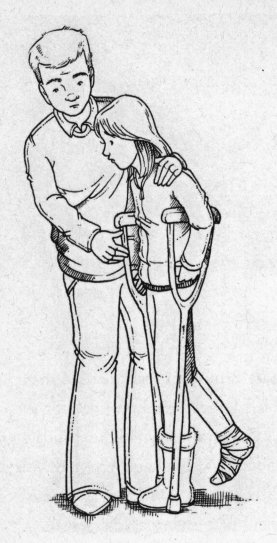

could be a lot worse."

"No, they couldn't," Sara said glumly.
She flicked back her shoulder-length

brown hair as she arranged her long legs across the seat. "The auditions are next week. Why did this have to happen to me?"

Jane Lewis, her dance teacher, was going to choose four of her best students to form a team that would train together every week and eventually dance at local events.

"Accidents happen sometimes, I'm afraid." Sara's mom got into the driver's side. She glanced into the rearview mirror and gave her daughter a sympathetic smile. "Cheer up, sweetheart. There'll be lots of other opportunities."

Not like this, Sara thought glumly.

She really wanted to develop her dancing skills and become a more confident performer. Being part of a regular team would have been perfect for her.

Sara stared fixedly out of the side window at the familiar streets as her mom drove them home, but in her mind she was back at the studio with all her dance friends. Just a couple of hours ago, she was enjoying the wonderful feeling of her body moving in time to the music as she learned some new steps.

Then it had happened. She'd landed awkwardly, slipped onto the side of her foot, and felt a sharp pain zing through her ankle. The doctor had told her she'd sprained it, and even though it didn't hurt that much now that it was all bandaged up, she'd been told that if she wanted it to heal properly she had to rest it completely.

That meant no dancing for three whole weeks!

Despite Sara's efforts to put on a brave face, her eyes pricked with tears.

"I wonder what Beth's going to do now?" her dad remarked. "You two practically live at that studio."

"I know. I feel really bad for her," Sara said miserably.

She and Beth were best friends as well as dance partners. They'd been practicing an awesome new routine for Jane's auditions. Now Beth would have to perform it on her own.

Sara remembered something. "I left some of my stuff in the lockers at the studio. Could we go and get it, please?"

"Are you sure you want to? I can get it for you anytime," her mom offered.

Sara shook her head. "Dance classes will have finished for the day, so I can just go in quickly without everyone making a fuss. Anyway, I might as well start getting used to these things." She waved one of the crutches.

Her mom nodded. "Okay."

A few minutes later, they parked outside the community college. It was an impressive dome-shaped building, always flooded with light from the glass panels that formed its walls. Its wide staircase and high ceiling could be seen through the entrance windows.

Sara's dad helped her out of the car. He walked with her through the automatic front doors and then they took the elevator together up to the first floor. Adults and kids wearing workout clothes passed them in the hallway. The smell of freshly brewed coffee met them as they approached the large open-plan café.

"I'll be fine now, Dad. The studio's just over there. Why don't you wait here for me?"

"If you're sure," he said, taking a seat in the café. "Be careful on those crutches."

"I will." Sara negotiated the door into the changing rooms next to the studio. She managed to get across the room, but it was difficult to fish her locker key out of her jeans pocket while balancing on crutches.

She carefully propped one of them against the lockers, so she had a hand free. Opening her locker, she reached for a book, an MP3 player, and some practice clothes and began stuffing them into a spare bag that she found crumpled at the back. It was a bit awkward with one hand, but she finally managed it.

As she closed the locker, she didn't notice that she'd brushed against the crutch that was propped next to her. It slid sideways and crashed to the ground. The loud noise made Sara almost jump

out of her skin, and she dropped the bag in surprise.

"Oh great! Now what do I do?" she groaned.

There was no point in calling for her dad, as he wouldn't hear her through two doors. She'd have to try to bend down to pick up the crutch herself.

"Right. How hard can this be?"

Sara gritted her teeth. Keeping her injured ankle in the air, she balanced on one crutch and tried to crouch down. But then she lost her balance and felt herself falling.

"Oh!" she gasped as she braced herself for a painful landing.

Suddenly, there was a bright flash and a cloud of crystal dust appeared and swirled around Sara. She felt a strange warm tingling sensation down her spine, but the hard bump she expected never came.

To her complete amazement, Sara found herself hovering in midair a few inches above the floor. She caught her breath as she felt herself turning and then floating gently downward until she ended up sitting on the floor with her long legs outstretched.

"What just happened?" She felt like pinching herself to see if she was dreaming.

"I hope you are not hurt?" asked a little voice from across the changing room.

Chapter
TWO

Sara looked around and saw a tiny,
fluffy black-and-white bunny crouching
on top of the nearest bench. It had big
chocolate-brown eyes, and they seemed
to be twinkling with tiny rainbows. Sara's
eyes widened as she tried to make sense of
what had just happened. She must be more
shaken up by her fall than she thought.
She was imagining the strangest things!

Sara watched as the cute bunny hopped closer toward her—it was definitely real. But there was no way it could have spoken to her!

"How did you get in here?" she thought aloud. "I wonder if you belong to someone from the dance class?"

"I do not belong to anyone," the bunny told her. "I had just arrived here when I saw you fall, so I used my magic to stop you from hurting yourself. I am sorry if I startled you."

Sara did a double take. "You . . . you really can talk!" she blurted out.

The bunny blinked at her. Despite its tiny size, it didn't seem to be afraid of her.

Sara noticed that it wore a tiny gold key on a chain around its neck.

"All the rabbits in my warren can talk. I am Arrow, guardian of Moonglow Meadow and keeper of the key that keeps our meadow lush and green," the bunny said, lifting his fluffy little head proudly. "May I know your name?"

"S-Sara. Sara Penfold. I just . . . um . . . came in here to . . . erm . . . pick up some of my stuff," she stammered. Her mind was still whirling. She couldn't believe this was happening, but she didn't want to scare this amazing bunny away.

"Thanks for saving me from hurting myself. I could have made my bad ankle even worse."

"You are welcome!" Arrow bowed his head. "I am honored to meet you, Sara."

"Um . . . me too." She dipped her head, feeling a bit strange at being so formal while still sitting on the floor with only one sneaker on and a heavily bandaged ankle.

Arrow twitched his long floppy ears and his face took on a serious look. "I need somewhere to hide, and quickly."

"Why do you need to do that?" Sara asked. "Is someone after you?"

The black-and-white bunny's brown eyes flashed with sadness and anger.

"Yes. I am in hiding from our neighbors, who are fierce dark rabbits.

Their land is dry and stony, but they refuse to share our meadow with us. They want to steal the key and use it to make their own land green again. If they do this, Moonglow Meadow will become a desert."

"Oh no! That would be terrible!" Sara exclaimed.

"Yes, it would. That is why Strike, our leader, sent me here to keep the magic key safe."

Sara frowned, puzzled. "Is Moonglow Meadow near here then—behind the community college?"

The tiny bunny shook his head. "It is far away. In another world."

Sara felt her curiosity taking over from her shock. Arrow's homeland sounded so strange and wonderful! "No offense, but you're very tiny for such an important mission," she said gently.

Rainbows gleamed more brightly in Arrow's dewy brown eyes. "Please stay there," he ordered, rising up onto his back legs.

Sara felt another warm prickling sensation down her spine as the key around Arrow's neck began flashing and a cloud of shimmering crystal dust appeared. It swirled around him like a miniature whirlwind, and when it cleared, Sara saw that the cute black-and-white bunny had disappeared. In his place stood the most beautiful and impressive rabbit she had ever seen. It was the size of a large cat and had silky pure-white fur, flecked with silver. The tips of his large ears looked as if they'd been dipped in silver glitter and

his glowing chocolate-brown eyes flashed
with jewel-bright rainbows.

"Arrow?" Sara gasped in wonderment.

"Yes, it is still me, Sara," Arrow said in
a smooth, velvety voice.

Before she had time to get over the
shock of seeing Arrow in his true form,
there was a final flash of bright light
from the key around his neck and he

reappeared as a tiny, fluffy black-and-white bunny.

"Wow! That's a really cool disguise."

Arrow shook his head. "The dark rabbits will see through it if any of them find me. I must hide now. Can you help me, please?"

"Yes! You can live with me!" Sara decided without a second thought. "We've got a big garden with lots of grass and stuff to eat. Just wait until I tell Mom and Dad about you. And Beth, she's my best friend. No one's going to believe it!"

"No, I am sorry, Sara. You cannot tell anyone about me," Arrow said seriously. "You must promise me."

Sara felt disappointed, especially about not telling her best friend. She and Beth always told each other everything. But if it would help to keep the magic bunny safe, then she was prepared to make an exception.

"Okay then. Cross my heart. I'll have to smuggle you into our house somehow. I know, you can get into my bag . . ."

"Sara?" a voice called out. "Are you all right? You've been a long time in there." Sara froze and then quickly turned her head to see her dad coming into the changing room. A horrified look crossed his face as he saw her sitting on the floor.

"Oh my goodness! Have you hurt yourself? I knew I should have come in with you!"

"I'm fine. Really," Sara reassured him. "I landed on my bottom, not my bad ankle. But then I couldn't reach the crutches to get up again."

From the corner of her eye, she saw Arrow leap off the bench, hop toward the open bag lying on the floor, and crawl inside it. But for some reason her dad didn't seem to notice.

"Do you have everything you wanted from your locker? Then let's get you back on your feet!" Her dad helped her get up and balance on her crutches and then he picked up the bag with Arrow inside it.

"Thanks, Dad. Let's go. Mom must be wondering where we've gone," Sara said as she limped toward the door. All she wanted to do was get Arrow safely back home and then settle in with her secret bunny friend.

Chapter
THREE

When they got home, Sara struggled
up to her room, closed the door, and put
her bag on the bed. Arrow immediately
jumped out and sat on the blanket.

He looked around her room with
bright, intelligent eyes.

Sara sat next to him. "How come
Dad didn't see you get into my bag?"
she asked, stroking the bunny's fluffy

black-and-white fur.

"I used my magic so that only you will be able to see and hear me," Arrow told her, his whiskers twitching.

"You can make yourself invisible? Cool! That's going to make it much easier for me to take you out with me."

Arrow nodded. "This is a safe place. I think I will be happy here," he said. He yawned sleepily and rubbed his eyes with one fluffy paw.

Sara smiled at him fondly. It must have been a long journey for the tiny bunny. She began tucking the duvet around him like a cozy nest.

"There you are. Now you can have a nap." She kissed the top of his head, breathing in the sweet smell of his warm fur.

"Thank you, Sara." Arrow tucked his nose between his front paws. Almost immediately his breathing changed and snuffly bunny snores rose from his little body.

Just then the phone rang in the hall downstairs. Sara heard her mom answer it and footsteps sounded on the stairs. Her mom poked her head around the door to hand Sara the phone.

"It's Beth for you, sweetie."

"Thanks, Mom." Sara took the phone from her eagerly, pleased that her best friend had called. "Hi, Beth."

"Sara! How's your ankle? I was so worried about you. Everyone in dance class wants to know if you're okay. Your mom told me you just got back from the hospital. Do you have a plaster cast?"

"No. Just a bandage. My ankle's badly sprained."

Beth gave a sigh of relief. "That's not so bad then. You'll have to miss a couple of classes, but we can do extra practice at my house to make up for it. We're totally going to win a place in Jane's new team!" she said confidently.

Despite herself, Sara grinned. Beth's confidence was one of the things she liked best about her.

"Sorry, Beth, but I won't be able to dance for at least three weeks. That's how long it's going to take for my ankle to heal. I won't be able to make the auditions," she said quietly.

"Oh no!" Beth exclaimed. "That's too bad. I'd *really* set my heart on joining Jane's team."

"Tell me about it," Sara said glumly, her spirits sinking. "I've messed things up for both of us, haven't I?"

Finding Arrow had taken her mind off her injury for a little while. But now she realized again how much it affected their dance dreams, both hers *and* Beth's.

"You can't help it. It's just bad luck," Beth said generously. "Hang on, Mom's calling me. I'm going to visit my grandmother for the weekend." She covered the phone with her hand and yelled, "I'm coming!" then spoke to Sara again. "You'll be at school on Monday, though, right? I'll see you then!"

"Yup. Have a good time at your grandmother's. Bye, Beth." Sara put the phone down on her bedside table.

She sighed. She'd expected Beth to visit so they could at least talk and maybe look at some dancing magazines together.

It was going to be a long weekend
without her best friend around to cheer
her up.

Sara looked down at the tiny fluffy
black-and-white bunny. Arrow's little
sides were moving up and down and
his whiskers were twitching as if he was
dreaming. He was so cute—and so brave
to have come here all by himself.

Maybe they could help each other to
feel less lonely.

"I love having you living with me!"
Sara said to Arrow on Monday morning.
Even normal things like having breakfast,
doing homework in her bedroom, and
watching TV were fun when you had
a magical friend for company. She'd
spent quite a bit of time with him in

the garden, throwing small twigs for him
to bring back to her or cuddling him
while she read.

Arrow's ears twitched. "I like it here
with you, too."

"Ready to get inside?" Sara smiled at
him as she finished packing her school
bag.

Arrow nodded and jumped straight in.

Sara's mom gave them a ride to school.
Beth came dashing up the road just as Sara
reached the school gate. "Hi, Sara!" she
puffed.

"Hi, Beth." Sara smiled happily as her
friend ran up. She was a bit puzzled about
why she was so out of breath. Beth was
usually there first and waiting to meet her.

She'd been a bit worried that Beth
would be annoyed with her for not

being able to dance their routine for the audition. But Beth seemed her usual self as she chatted on their way to class about her weekend with her grandma.

"So, what did you do?" Beth asked finally.

"Oh, not much really," Sara said vaguely. Beth wouldn't have believed her even if she could have told her about the invisible fluffy bunny that was leaning up and looking out of her school bag.

When the bell rang, they walked into class together.

The first lesson was math, which wasn't Sara's favorite subject. She chewed the end of her pen and looked up from her workbook to see what Arrow was doing. His little black-and-white form appeared for a moment between two desks, before he disappeared under them again.

Sara smiled to herself, imagining his little pink nose snuffling up all the interesting smells. After a few minutes, he reappeared from beneath the desk and she saw him making for the nature table.

Arrow reared up onto his back legs to investigate a branch drooping over the side. He nibbled a bit of leaf and seemed to like the taste. His fluffy tail twitched eagerly as he took a firmer grip and started to pull.

"Uh-oh!" Sara breathed.

Birds' nests, leaves, and dried plants in empty jam jars that were entangled with the branch began to slide toward the edge of the table. The whole thing was going to tumble onto the tiny bunny at any moment, but Sara was too far away to warn Arrow.

What was she going to do?

Chapter
FOUR

"*Ah-cho-oo-oo!*" Sara sneezed as noisily as possible. "*Hrr-up! Splurgh!*" she coughed.

Beside her, Beth dropped her pencil in surprise.

The teacher frowned and gave Sara a disapproving look. "What's wrong, Sara? Do you need a glass of water?"

"Sorry, Miss!" Sara apologized. "I almost . . . um . . . swallowed a fly! I'm fine now."

Her classmates giggled, especially Beth.

But it had done the trick. Across the
classroom, the noise had made Arrow
jump backward from the table in fright.
His magic key glowed brightly and he
landed on Sara's desk in a *whoosh* of crystal

dust. His fur was all on end and his body looked as round as a soft, fuzzy ball.

"Are you okay?" Sara whispered to him, as everyone went back to work.

"I am fine now," Arrow told her, shaking himself so his black-and-white fur settled back down. "What happened?"

"You were about to pull all that stuff on top of you. I had to do something," she explained. "It's probably best if you don't nibble things in class. You could get into all kinds of trouble. We'll be going outside at lunchtime, so you can eat some grass then."

"I did wrong. I am a bad bunny." Arrow buried his face in his front paws.

Sara's heart melted, and she barely managed to stop herself picking him up and giving him a cuddle. "No, you're not! You're my brave little friend," she whispered.

"Thank you, Sara." Arrow hunched down next to her pencil case.

"When's lunchtime? I'm starving!" Beth whispered loudly a few minutes later. She sat back and stretched her arms. "Must be all the extra practice we did . . . I mean . . . *I* did this morning. Oh, sorry . . ." her voice trailed off, raising her eyebrows apologetically. "I don't suppose you want to hear about that."

"It's okay," Sara told her with a grin. "I know I can't dance, but I'm not going to get upset if we talk about it. We did come up with a great routine, didn't we? It's such a shame we won't be performing it for Jane's audition."

"Um . . . yeah," Beth said, going red. Ducking her head, she fiddled about in her fake-fur pencil case.

Sara frowned, puzzled. Beth was acting strangely.

Just then, the lunch bell rang. Chairs scraped on the floor and desk drawers banged as everyone began filing out of the classroom. "It's probably best if you get into my bag," Sara whispered to Arrow.

"Okay." With a whisk of his tail, he jumped straight in.

Beth reached behind the desk for Sara's crutches. "Here you go."

"Thanks." Sara stood up and adjusted her weight on the crutches. She had slipped the long strap of her bag over one shoulder, so it hung across her body. That way she could be sure Arrow wasn't jostled about too much as she limped along.

Sara and Beth found a spare bench outside and opened their lunch boxes. Arrow hopped out of the bag and streaked across the grass.

Beth handed Sara a cupcake in a frilly wrapper. It had a lemon candy slice on top. "Mom made cupcakes. I brought you one."

"Thanks! Looks yummy!" Beth's mom was a great cook.

When they'd finished eating, they watched some girls practicing dance moves. Sara knew most of them from her dance class. One of them, a tall blond-haired girl named Olya, was a really good dancer.

"Hiya!" Olya called, smiling and waving as she saw Sara watching.

Sara waved back. She turned to say something to Beth and saw her smiling widely and giving the blond girl a double thumbs-up. It looked as if Olya had been waving at Beth and not Sara.

Sara was puzzled. What was going on? She didn't think Beth and Olya were all that friendly.

Beth turned to watch some girls who were doing complicated dance moves. Sara saw Beth nodding her head in time to the imaginary music and doing some of the arm movements in time with the other girls. Olya motioned to her to join them.

Beth jumped to her feet eagerly and looked at Sara. "Do you mind?"

"Of course not. Go ahead," Sara said. She watched them wistfully, hating having to just sit there. Beth, Olya, and the other girls were having so much fun doing more and more complicated moves.

Sighing, she hoped it wouldn't be too long before her ankle healed and she could dance again.

Arrow had finished eating grass. He hopped back across the playing field toward the bench where Sara sat and stopped beside it to groom himself.

Beth was fooling around, doing a moonwalk as the others clapped. She glided smoothly across the grass as if she was sliding on ice.

Sara tensed. Beth was moving closer to where Arrow sat. He was so busy licking his pale tummy that he hadn't noticed the danger. Any second now, Beth was going to step on her invisible little friend!

"Look out!" she cried, lifting one crutch. She only meant to wave it warningly, but before she could swing it out of the way, Beth tripped over it.

"Ow!" Beth sprawled full length on the grass.

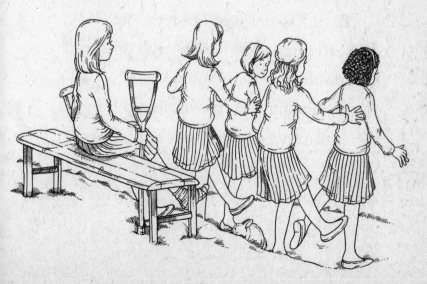

Startled, Arrow leaped in the air and
quickly hopped under the bench out of
harm's way.

Beth scrambled to her feet. She
brushed grass off her uniform. "What did
you do that for?" she shouted.

"I thought you were going to hurt
Arr— I mean, bash into my ankle," Sara
quickly corrected, horrified that she'd
almost given away Arrow's secret. She
would have to be more careful.

"I saw what happened. You tripped Beth on purpose," Olya cried. "You're jealous because Beth's asked me to be her new dance partner!"

Sara looked up in total disbelief as the tall girl strode toward her, her blond hair swinging out behind her.

Chapter
FIVE

Sara gaped at her best friend. "Beth?
What's Olya talking about? I'm your
dance partner!"

"I was going to tell you," Beth said,
looking sheepish. "I just really wanted
to audition for the dance team, but our
routine doesn't work as a solo. So I . . . I
asked Olya to dance it with me instead.
That's okay, isn't it?" she said quietly. "It's

only while your ankle's getting better. You're still my usual dance partner."

Sara knew how much winning a place on Jane's new team meant to Beth. But she had assumed that Beth wouldn't go for it without her. What would happen if Beth got a place and Sara didn't? She swallowed hard, trying not to feel upset.

"All right," she said, nodding slowly.

"Thanks, Sara!" Beth sounded relieved. "I've been putting off telling you, 'cause I was worried that you'd be angry with me."

"No way! We've been friends forever." Sara managed a smile, despite the sinking feeling in her tummy at being left out. If Beth and Olya joined Jane's new team, they'd be practicing hard and taking extra classes, but she wouldn't be included. Would Beth still be her best friend?

"It's a great routine," Olya said. "You and Beth must have worked really hard on it. I'm going to dance it the best I can. And I'm sorry for what I said about you tripping Beth and stuff."

Sara shrugged. "That's okay." Olya actually seemed quite nice. Another time, she would have enjoyed dancing with her and Beth. She just hoped that Beth wouldn't like Olya so much that she

decided to become best friends with her instead. Maybe when Sarah's ankle was better they could all team up.

The bell rang again, and everyone began crowding back into school. Sara's spirits sank a bit as she thought of having to sit around while Beth and Olya had all the fun.

Arrow hopped up to Sara's school bag and leaped inside. His big brown eyes shone with affection. "Thank you for stopping Beth from stepping on me."

"I'd say we're even!" she whispered back. "*You* saved *me* from hurting myself when I fell over in the changing room."

Arrow nodded, his little nose twitching. "It is good that friends can help each other."

Sara smiled at him as she shouldered

her bag and felt herself starting to cheer up a little. The magic bunny was her very own special secret—she would never share him with anyone.

Two days later, Sara and Arrow were sitting in an empty classroom. It was a cool, rather windy day. From outside came the sounds of voices and laughter from the tennis courts and playing fields.

Sara sighed glumly. The teacher had suggested she stay inside to keep warm, so she was catching up on some reading for their class project. But she just couldn't get interested in reading about Vikings today.

"I'm fed up with limping around on these dumb crutches. I can't do anything exciting," she grumbled, closing the book with a thud.

Sara tried to make a big effort to cheer herself up for Arrow's sake. He didn't deserve such a grumpy friend. She fished a scrap of paper out of her pencil case, scrunched it up, and then flicked it across her desk.

Arrow's eyes gleamed brightly. One tiny fluffy front paw shot out, and he trapped the paper beneath it.

"Wow! Great reflexes!" Sara was impressed. "Let's test them some more."

Arrow looked up at her in puzzlement. "How are we going to do that?"

"I've got an idea." Sara collected a few books and then stacked them at intervals on the nearby work surface. She propped others up to make a tunnel. "There you go. A bunny obstacle course!"

Arrow's whiskers twitched eagerly as

he hopped to one end of the course.

"Go, Arrow! Go, Arrow!" Sara encouraged in a singsong voice. "Go, Arrow!"

Flattening his ears, the magic bunny hopped forward. He jumped over the obstacles and ducked through the tunnel, his cottontail flicking delightedly.

Sara hobbled to one end of the work surface. Propping her crutches against a nearby desk, she opened her arms as Arrow hopped over the last pile of books. He gave a mighty leap and launched himself right at her.

Sara caught him and gave him a

big hug. She kissed the top of his fluffy head. "Yay! This beats playing outside. You'd definitely get a place in the bunny Olympics!"

"It was lots of fun!" Arrow agreed, gently touching her chin with his pink nose.

"Come on. Let's go for a walk to the coatroom and back. Most kids are outside, so you can hop around for a change without worrying about being stepped on."

She picked up her crutches and they set off down the hallway. As they reached another empty classroom, Sara thought she saw something moving. The door was partly open, so she stopped to look.

There was a girl dancing in the center of the room. She was slim with striking dark-red hair and pale skin and looked about ten years old—a year or so older than Sara. Sara couldn't remember ever seeing the girl in the playground.

"I wonder who she is," she whispered to Arrow.

They stood in the doorway silently watching as the girl danced around the room. She was doing a series of complicated spins, twists, and locks.

"Wow! She's *really* good!" Sara whispered, totally spellbound as the girl finished her routine with a graceful downward sweep of one arm. She couldn't contain herself any longer. Pushing the door wide open, she went in. "That was amazing! Where did you learn to dance like that?" she exclaimed.

The girl whipped around, a look of

shock on her face. "Oh! I . . . I didn't
know anyone was there!" she said,
flustered. "I didn't mean to . . . Sorry,
I've . . . um . . . gotta go!" As she grabbed
her bag from a nearby desk, something
fell to the floor. But in her haste, the girl
didn't notice.

"Hey, wait!" Sara started forward as the
girl dashed away toward a door in the far
corner of the room. "What's your name?"

There was no answer. The girl had left.

Arrow hopped into the room and

went over to the crumpled object on the floor. Grasping it in his teeth, he dragged it over to Sara.

"Thanks, Arrow. Look, it's a gym shirt." She read the name tag. "Tamara Blake. I wonder why she ran away like that?"

Arrow shook his head. "I do not know."

Sara nodded in agreement. "Strange, wasn't it? If I could dance like that, I'd be really proud of myself." She draped the gym shirt over a chair before she and Arrow continued on their walk.

Chapter SIX

After school finished for the day, Sara and Arrow waited for Beth by the main gate. "Beth's coming home with us tonight. Mom's treating us to a pizza," Sara told Arrow.

"What is *pizza*?" Arrow's whiskers twitched in curiosity.

"It's sort of flat bread with tomatoes and other stuff, topped with melted cheese. Wait until you taste it. You'll love it!" She decided to ask for one with lots of spinach, especially for Arrow.

Arrow licked his lips. "I like trying new human food."

Sara smiled as she stroked his soft little front paws that were poking out from her school bag. "I can't decide whether to tell

Beth about Tamara," she mused, changing the subject.

Arrow looked up at her, a tiny rainbow gleaming in each big brown eye. "Tamara might not want anyone to know she was dancing by herself."

Sara thought Arrow could be right. She didn't even know the red-haired girl, but there was something about her that she liked, and she didn't feel right about tattling on her.

She chewed at her lip. "I know," she agreed, "but Beth's my best friend. We usually tell each other everything. It feels strange to keep secrets from her."

Arrow lifted a paw and placed it on her hand. "It is not your secret. It is Tamara's," he said quietly.

Sara smiled at her wise friend. "You're

right! Let's keep this just between you and me for now."

"Sara!" Beth came out of school. She waved and quickened her steps as she hurried toward Sara and Arrow. "I hope you weren't too bored all by yourself while we were playing tennis."

"Oh, I found lots to do," Sara said vaguely. *Like having fun with my magic bunny friend and finding a mystery dancer!* "Mom's over there. Let's go!"

"Um . . . sorry, Sara," Beth said, wrinkling her nose in apology. "But I can't come for a pizza after all. I've got to meet Olya. We're doing extra practice in the evenings all week."

"What, *every* evening?" Sara said, surprised. "And sometimes before school, too?"

"Yes, Olya wants to be the best she can for Jane's auditions," Beth said reasonably.

Sara nodded, not very happy about it. Beth was her best friend after all, and she wasn't used to having to share her. "I suppose I'd want to do extra practice if it was me," she said reluctantly. "Well—see you tomorrow at school."

"Sure. Bye!" Beth said, walking away.

Sara waved, knowing that Beth's mind already was on her dancing.

Sighing, she felt her thoughts turning to Tamara. How odd that Beth and Olya were rehearsing so much in public and yet someone as talented as Tamara Blake chose to hide away and dance by herself in an empty classroom.

It didn't make sense.

"Mm-mm. Mushrooms, olives, and extra spinach with a cheesy stuffed crust. This is the best!" Sara and Arrow sat in the garden. She helped herself to another slice from the open box.

Beth might not be here, but it was fun to share with Arrow and especially watch him enjoying his very first taste of pizza.

Sara folded a long string of mozzarella into her mouth. "I've got a new DVD of Shanilla Jakes. She's one of my favorite performers. We could watch it together," she suggested.

Arrow nodded, still munching. "'I would like that."

"Come on then. I'll ask to borrow

Mom's laptop. You and I can cuddle up together on my bed and watch it!"

Her mom carried the laptop upstairs for her. Arrow stretched out full-length beside her on the bed. Sara loaded the DVD, and the screen filled with colorful images.

Arrow's little face lit up in wonder. "How is this world trapped in a box?" he asked, his whiskers tickling her fingers.

It was a difficult question, and Sara tried to explain.

"Well—those moving pictures were filmed from real life. But what we're watching is like a memory—kind of. I don't really know how DVDs work," she admitted with a grin. "I just enjoy watching them. Wow! Look at the way Shanilla Jakes moves! Isn't she great?

"I wish I could dance like that."

Arrow looked up at her with rainbow-bright brown eyes. "I am sure you will be a very good dancer one day."

"Thanks, Arrow," she said, smiling at her loyal friend. "I know it would help me to get better if I got a place on Jane's new team. Oh well. There's no point in complaining about it." Sara felt a pang of sadness as she thought about Beth and Olya rehearsing together right now.

"Is there not another dance team you could join?" Arrow asked, rubbing his fluffy cheek against her arm.

Sara stroked his velvety ears. "I don't think so. Not around here anyway. Someone else might start one up. You never know," she said hopefully.

Lights flashed and created dramatic

shadows in the music video playing on the
laptop. For a second, the shadows merged
together and made a strange rabbit-shaped
image on the screen.

Arrow gave a squeal of fright. "My
enemies have found me!" he cried.

"What? Where?" Sara said, puzzled.
"Oh, you mean that rabbit-shaped shadow
on the—"

Arrow wasn't listening. Leaping onto
the floor, he shot straight toward the open
bedroom door. To Sara's horror, he rushed

outside, and she heard his nails scrabbling on the wooden stairs.

"Oh no!" she gasped. There was no telling where he'd go in his panic.

She clambered down from the bed. Not wanting to waste time reaching for her crutches, she hopped after the terrified bunny on one leg. Holding the railing, Sara followed him downstairs as quickly as she could.

The sound of the TV came from the sitting room. Luckily, her parents were watching their favorite television program.

"Arrow! Stop!" Sara hissed, not daring to raise her voice in case her mom and dad came out to ask what she was doing without her crutches.

Steadying herself on the wall, she went into the kitchen and glimpsed Arrow's

cottontail through the open back door as
he shot under the patio table. Sara went
outside and lowered herself awkwardly
to the ground. Arrow was tucked into
a tight ball behind the table leg. She
crawled toward him and gently picked
him up.

"It's okay. There are no bad rabbits
here," she crooned, cuddling him in her
arms. "It was just a trick of the light.
DVDs aren't real, remember?"

But Arrow was still trembling and
didn't seem to have heard her.

Sara felt a tingling sensation down
her spine as his key flashed and a crystal
cloud appeared. It surrounded her and
Arrow and shimmered as it turned into
something fluffy and squishy that felt like
a huge soft comforter.

"Oh!" To Sara's total amazement,
she felt herself floating upward with
Arrow next to her. They were hovering
high in the air on a soft sparkling white
cloud, out of sight of anyone below! The
old apple tree in the backyard was far
below them, and the neighboring yards
were spread out like brightly colored
patchwork.

Sara glanced at Arrow, who crouched next to her, peeking over the pillowy edge. His whiskers twitched nervously as he searched for signs of his enemies.

"See? There are no dark rabbits anywhere, or you'd be able to see them from way up here," she reassured him gently. "Now do you believe me?"

He nodded slowly. "You are right, Sara. I am sorry I panicked." His long floppy ears drooped. "I must try to be brave."

"You are brave," Sara said gently. "And you can do the most amazing things, too! I can't believe we're up here—I've never thought that our house and garden could look so beautiful!"

As she looked at him, the key around his neck began flashing more brightly than she'd ever seen it.

"Moonglow Meadow will soon be in need of the key's power," Arrow told her.

Sara's chest tightened with panic. "Do . . . do you have to leave right now?" she asked worriedly.

"No. Not until the key glows steadily. Then I will know that its magic is needed urgently. If that happens, I will have to leave at once, maybe without saying good-bye."

Sara knew that she would have to be very strong if that happened, but she couldn't bear to think of it right now. She decided to try to enjoy every moment she could with Arrow.

Just as Sara was wondering where else she and Arrow might be able to go on their magical sparkling cloud, she heard a noise below.

"Sara?" It was her mom's voice coming from the house as she called upstairs. "I'm going to make a cold drink. I'll bring one up to you!"

Chapter SEVEN

Sara stiffened. "Oh no! Mom thinks I'm still watching the DVD. She's going to wonder where I am when she goes into my bedroom. What should I do?"

"Do not worry. We'll float back in through your bedroom window before she notices. But I have used my magic, so we have a little time to spare. I thought you might like to enjoy being able to float on this cloud with me for a while."

"Oh yes. It's so . . . magical. Better than anything!"

"Better than dancing?" Arrow asked teasingly.

She grinned. "Nothing's better than dancing. But this is close!"

Sara looked around. From high up above the tree, she could see across all the backyards down the street.

Two gardens away, she spotted a small figure on a lawn. It was a girl with dark red hair, and she was dancing.

Sara narrowed her eyes as she felt a surge of excitement. "I think that's Tamara Blake! I wondered why I hadn't seen her around. Her family must have just moved into that empty house. Let's go closer. Will she be able to see us?"

"No, I used my magic so we are both invisible."

Arrow and Sara gently floated toward the garden where Tamara was dancing. Once again, just like in the classroom, Tamara seemed lost in her own private world of dance. She dipped and spun and struck graceful poses.

A younger girl, who looked very like Tamara, came out of the house. The

moment Tamara glimpsed her sister, she
stopped dancing. She quickly grabbed a
book that was sitting nearby on a table
and pretended to be reading.

Sara frowned, puzzled. "Tamara
really hates anyone seeing her dancing.
I wonder if it's because she's shy," she
said thoughtfully. "Going to dance
classes every week helped me feel more
confident. Maybe they'd help her, too."

"You could tell her about them,"
Arrow suggested.

Sara hadn't thought that far ahead. But
maybe Arrow was right.

Arrow's brown eyes suddenly lit up
with urgency. "We must leave! It is time
for you to be back in your bedroom."

Everything seemed to go into fast
forward. As the sparkling magical cloud

whooshed downward, Sara and Arrow
bounced on its billowy surface. They
reached her window in the blink of an
eye. Sara giggled as she felt a ticklish
stretching sensation, and they whooshed
in through her open window.

She landed in a heap on her bed and
the sparkling cloud dissolved into sugary
dust around her and disappeared. Sara
ran a hand through her tousled hair and
quickly sat up just as her mom walked
into the room holding a tray.

"Here you are. I've brought you a snack as well."

"Thanks, Mom."

Sara glanced at Arrow, who was nestled against her pillow. *That was close,* she thought, biting back a grin. Floating on a cloud with her magic bunny friend was the best fun ever!

Chapter EIGHT

Saturday morning dawned bright and clear. Sara woke from a wonderful dream. She had been dancing in a forest, where every tree glittered with crystal droplets.

"I love how it feels when I dance. It's the best!" she said, stretching. "I've decided to go and watch Beth and Olya dance in the audition. It's no good moping around, just because I can't audition. And I know how much this means to Beth."

Arrow was curled up on the pillow near her shoulder. He opened one sleepy brown eye.

"You are a good friend to Beth. And a kind person, Sara."

"When I'm not grumpy, you mean?" She laughed wryly. "I've been thinking about Tamara, too. I'm going to try to find out why she dances in secret."

"How are you going to do that?" Arrow stretched out his front paws and then his back legs, before giving himself a shake.

Sara drew him gently into her arms and stroked his warm fur. "I need some way of getting her to talk to me. I've got an idea! How about if we . . ."

Arrow listened intently as Sara finished

explaining. He twitched his ears in agreement. "That is a good plan."

"Let's do it!" Sara threw back the duvet and reached for her clothes.

Straight after breakfast, she told her mom she was going to the corner store to buy some candy with her allowance. It wasn't exactly a lie, as Tamara's house was on the way.

"This is it," Sara whispered when they reached the front gate. "You know what to do."

Arrow's big brown eyes glinted with tiny rainbows. His magic key glowed brightly. "I am no longer invisible."

"Good. Ready?"

Arrow nodded. Hopping under the front gate, he hopped up the short path. Sara waited until her magic bunny was

hidden behind a large plant pot near
the front door. She took a deep breath,
hobbled up to the front door, and rang
the doorbell. There was a pause, and then
Tamara herself opened the door.

"Yes?" she said, smiling. She was even
prettier up close, with lovely hazel eyes.

"Hi! I'm . . . um . . . Sara Penfold. I
live just down the street. I'm looking for

my pet rabbit. He's escaped. I think he
might be in your front yard."

"Oh, the poor little thing. He must be
really scared. I'll help you look for him."
Tamara stepped outside. "What does he
look like?"

"Thanks." Sara smiled gratefully. "He's
tiny with fluffy black-and-white fur, a cute
pink nose, and huge chocolate-brown eyes."

Arrow saw his chance. He hopped
forward and paused for a second on the
path to make sure they saw him. Then
he slipped past Tamara and dashed into a
clump of flowers.

"There he is!" Tamara cried, running
after him. "I'll get him!"

Sara grinned to herself. The plan was
working!

Arrow flattened his ears and darted

about in circles, pretending to be a scared little tame bunny.

Tamara made a grab for him. "Got you!" she cried triumphantly.

"Phew!" Sara let out a big sigh of relief. "I didn't think I'd ever catch him."

"Hello, bunnykins," Tamara crooned. She held Arrow gently but firmly. "Isn't he gorgeous? His eyes are like melted chocolate with rainbow glitter mixed in. How long have you had him?"

"Not very long," Sara said vaguely. "But I love him to pieces. Thanks very much for helping me to catch him. He's called Arrow."

"Cool name." Tamara smiled, as she handed Arrow over. "Did you say you live just up the road? Do you go to Denton School?"

"Yes. I do. I think I saw you the other day," Sara said casually. "I walked past an empty classroom. And you were dancing—"

"That was you?" Tamara interrupted, blushing.

"Yes. I dance, too. Well—I did, before I hurt my ankle. I go to dance classes at the community college with my best friend, Beth," Sara rushed on quickly, hoping that Tamara would stay and listen to her this time. "Jane Lewis, the teacher, is really nice. She's starting a new dance team. Beth and I were planning to audition together to win a place."

"That's bad luck," Tamara said. "You must be really disappointed."

"I was for a while," Sara admitted. "Beth's still going to dance our routine.

She's asked Olya, another girl from our class, to be her partner. The auditions are tomorrow. I'm going to go and cheer them on. Would you like to come with me?"

"Me?" Tamara said, surprised. "I . . . I don't know."

"It'll be fun," Sara encouraged. "And everyone is really friendly."

"I really used to love dancing and performing, but I was bullied for showing off at my old school," Tamara said quietly.

Suddenly everything made sense. Sara felt annoyed on Tamara's behalf.

"I hate kids like that! I bet they were jealous because you're so good. We're not like that here. *I'm* not like that. You'll see. If you come to the auditions, you can meet everyone, and then maybe you'd like to come to dance classes with me sometime?"

Tamara seemed to be considering it. "I've really missed dancing with other people. Maybe it's time I gave it another try. And I'd like to make some new friends around here." A slow smile spread over her face. "Okay, then."

"Fantastic! My mom's taking me. We'll

pick you up at five-thirty tomorrow."

"I'll be ready."

At the front gate, Sara turned and waved to Tamara. "Bye!" She looked at Arrow as they headed home. "Well done, Arrow. You were great. Our plan worked perfectly."

"I am glad. I like Tamara." He nuzzled her hand.

Sara rubbed the soft place between his ears. "Me too. I hope she'll like Beth and Olya. It would be great to have another dance friend."

Chapter
NINE

"I hope Tamara hasn't changed her mind about coming with us," Sara said to Arrow the following day.

But she didn't need to worry. Tamara was waiting outside her house when they drove up in her mom's car. Sara grinned.

"Hi!" Tamara greeted Sara warmly. "Thanks for picking me up, Mrs. Penfold."

"You're welcome," Sara's mom said,
smiling.

"Hi, Tamara," Sara said as Tamara got
into the back and sat next to her and
Arrow. "I called Beth to tell her we're
coming. She's looking forward to meeting
you."

"Me too," Tamara said.

The roads were unusually busy and
they crawled along, waiting in endless
traffic jams. It seemed as if every set
of traffic lights was on red. Sara began
fidgeting with impatience.

"I wish we could go faster. We're going to be late," she whispered to Arrow.

"This traffic is bad," Mrs. Penfold said. "I'm going to try another way."

They made for the outskirts where the roads were a bit clearer. Sara breathed a sigh of relief. They might still make it, if they were lucky. But her mom had just crossed a traffic circle when there was a loud *clunk*! The engine had cut out.

"Hold on, girls!" Mrs. Penfold cried, pressing a button to switch on the hazard lights. "I'm going to coast toward that curb." Moments later, they came to a stop.

"Oh no! Now we'll definitely miss Beth and Olya's dance!" Sara said unhappily.

"At least we're all okay. Your mom was great. She didn't panic or anything,"

Tamara said. "Mine would have freaked out!"

"Yeah, Mom's good at staying calm." Sara grinned, liking Tamara more and more as she spent more time with her.

Mrs. Penfold had spotted a rest stop, set back from the road. "We'll all go and sit over there, and I'll call for help."

They got out of the car. Sara began limping over to the wooden tables and benches on her crutches, with Arrow hopping beside her. Tamara was just ahead of them.

Sara felt a familiar warm tingling down her spine and noticed that Arrow's key was flashing and a small cloud of sparkly mist was drifting back toward the car. She turned to watch as it swirled around the hood before sinking into it and disappearing.

"You've fixed it for us! Thanks, Arrow.
You're a star!" Sara whispered.

"You are welcome," Arrow said
warmly.

"Come on!" Sara called to Tamara,
already hobbling back toward her mom,
who stood beside the car.

"Where are we going?" Tamara asked.

Sara didn't answer. She reached her
mom just as she had got out her phone to
call for help. "Mom! Wait! Try to start the
car again first!"

Mrs. Penfold blinked at her daughter in disbelief. "What are you talking about, sweetie? You saw what happened."

"I know. But I've got this really weird feeling. I *know* it will start. Just try it once more. *Please!*" Sara insisted.

Her mom shook her head slowly. "All right. But I don't know what good it will do," she said reluctantly.

She got back in and turned the key in the ignition. *Brrr-rrrrm!* It started like a rocket. "Would you believe it? It's just like magic!" Mrs. Penfold exclaimed in amazement.

Sara smiled, but stayed silent. She, Arrow, and Tamara piled back into the car, and they were soon on their way. This time there were no hold-ups. They reached the dance studio just as the doors opened and people began filing out.

"The auditions must have finished!" Sara realized with dismay. "I hope Beth and Olya haven't left yet. Let's go and see!"

Arrow looked out from her school bag as she went inside with Tamara at her side. She saw Beth and Olya sitting at one side of the studio, opposite the wall of full-length mirrors. Both of them looked downcast.

"What happened?" Sara asked Beth, although she thought she knew.

Beth sighed. "We didn't get picked," she said quietly. "Jane said it was a difficult choice because the standard was really high, but in the end she picked four other girls."

Olya shrugged. "There's always next time. It's not the end of the world."

"Isn't it?" Beth said glumly.

Sara felt a pang of disappointment for Beth. Mixed feelings swept through her. She felt sad for her competitive best friend, whose hopes had been dashed. But also relieved that Beth wasn't going to be spending lots of time training on a new team without her.

"I'm sorry, Beth. You and Olya couldn't have worked any harder," Sara said with feeling. She suddenly realized that Tamara was standing beside her. She was looking at the floor and fiddling with her hands. Maybe it wasn't the best time to introduce her, but they were here now. "This is Tamara. She just moved onto my street. She's a great dancer, and she's thinking about coming to dance classes with us."

"Hi, Tamara," Beth said, looking curious despite herself.

"Hi," Olya said.

"Sara told me about the auditions. I'm sorry you didn't make the team," Tamara said shyly.

"Thanks," Beth and Olya said together.

Suddenly, Beth stood up and linked arms with Sara. "Sorry to be such a grump. I'm sure there'll be other chances. How's your ankle feeling, anyway? I really miss dancing with you."

"Me too," Sara said happily, smiling at
her best friend. Her eyes sparkled. "But I'll
soon be back in my dancing shoes. Then,
watch out!"

Beth laughed, and Olya and Tamara
joined in.

Tamara's whole face had brightened. "I've decided—I'm definitely going to come to classes with all of you. It's going to be great to have some new dance fr—"

But Sara didn't hear the rest of what Tamara was saying because Arrow's key suddenly began to glow more brightly than she'd ever seen it. He leaped out of her bag in a whoosh of crystal dust that was twinkling with rainbow sparkles, and tore off down the hallway.

Sara's heart missed a beat. The moment she had been dreading was here!

Without a second thought, she hobbled after him and just caught a glimpse of him darting into a closet. She went in to find Arrow sitting there in his true form—a tiny fluffy black-and-white bunny no longer, but a magnificent rabbit

the size of a large cat. His silky pure-white
fur was flecked with silver, and his large
ears had glittering silver tips.

"Arrow!" Sara gasped. She'd forgotten
that her friend was so majestic. "You're
leaving right now, aren't you?"

Arrow's chocolate-brown eyes
softened with sadness. "Yes. Moonglow
Meadow urgently needs more of the
key's magic."

Sara nodded silently, her eyes
brimming with tears. She knew she had
to be brave and let him go. Arrow hopped
over and reared up on to his back legs,
so she could reach down to stroke him.
Her fingers brushed against his warm,
silky fur.

"I'll never forget you," she said, her
voice breaking.

"Nor I you. You have been a good friend, Sara." Arrow let her stroke him one final time and then moved away. "Farewell. Always follow your dreams," he said in a soft, velvety voice.

There was a final flash of light, and crystal dust trickled down around Sara and made a sound like the ringing of fairy bells as it hit the ground. Arrow faded and was gone.

Sara stood there, still not quite believing that she'd never see Arrow again. She swallowed her tears with an effort. Something lay on top of a nearby cardboard box. It was a single crystal rainbow drop. She reached out to pick it up. The drop tingled against her fingers as it turned into a tiny pure-white pebble in the shape of a bunny.

Sara slipped it into her pocket. She knew she would keep it forever as a reminder of the magic bunny and their time together. As she went out of the closet, Beth ran up to her.

"There you are! Tamara's great, isn't she? In fact, we were just talking, and I've had the best idea!"

Sara frowned. How come Beth looked so happy all of a sudden? "What idea?"

"To form *our own* dance team," Beth exclaimed. "The four of us—you, me, Olya, and Tamara. It's going to be awesome!"

Sara felt a smile spreading across her face. She knew that Arrow would be really pleased for her.

Say "hi" to the other magic bunnies for me. And look after Moonglow Meadow, she whispered under her breath.

Olya and Tamara came toward them with linked arms. Tamara was beaming with happiness.

"So, what are we going to call our team?" asked Olya.

"How about the Arrows?" Sara said happily.

About the
AUTHOR

Sue Bentley's books for children often include animals, fairies, and magic. She lives in Northampton, England, in a house surrounded by a hedge so she can pretend she's in the middle of the countryside. She loves reading and going to the movies, and writes while watching the birds on the feeders outside her window and eating chocolate. Sue grew up surrounded by small animals and loved them all—especially her gentle pet rabbits whose fur smelled so sweetly of rain and grass.

Don't miss these Magic Bunny books!

#1 Chocolate Wishes

#2 Vacation Dreams

#3 A Splash of Magic

#4 Classroom Capers

Don't miss these Magic Puppy books!

Don't miss these Magic Kitten books!

Don't miss these Magic Ponies books!